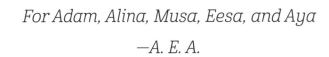

For Adam, Alina, Musa, Eesa, and Aya
—A. E. A.

For Daniel, who became my best friend,
even though he knew I am from another planet
—R. J. B.

SALAAM READS
An imprint of Simon & Schuster Children's Publishing Division
1230 Avenue of the Americas, New York, New York 10020
Text copyright © 2020 by Simon & Schuster, Inc.
Illustrations copyright © 2020 by Rahele Jomepour Bell
All rights reserved, including the right of reproduction in whole or in part in any form.
SALAAM READS and its logo are trademarks of Simon & Schuster, Inc.
For information about special discounts for bulk purchases, please contact Simon & Schuster Special Sales
at 1-866-506-1949 or business@simonandschuster.com.
The Simon & Schuster Speakers Bureau can bring authors to your live event. For more information or to book an event,
contact the Simon & Schuster Speakers Bureau at 1-866-248-3049 or visit our website at www.simonspeakers.com.
Book design by Laurent Linn
The text for this book was set in Cabrito.
The illustrations for this book were rendered using digital brushes and scanned, hand-printed textures.
Manufactured in China
0322 SCP
6 8 10 9 7
Library of Congress Cataloging-in-Publication Data
Names: Ali, A. E., author. | Bell, Rahele Jomepour, illustrator.
Title: Our favorite day of the year / A. E. Ali ; illustrated by Rahele Jomepour Bell.
Description: First edition. | New York : Salaam Reads, [2020] | Summary: Four kindergartners who think they have nothing in common
become friends after sharing traditions of their holidays, including Eid-ul-Fitr, Rosh Hashanah, Christmas, and Pi Day.
Identifiers: LCCN 2018051370 (print) | LCCN 2018055333 (eBook) |
ISBN 9781481485630 (hardcover) | ISBN 9781481485647 (eBook)
Subjects: | CYAC: Fasts and feasts—Fiction. | Friendship—Fiction. | Kindergarten—Fiction.
Classification: LCC PZ7.1.A4357 Mus 2020 (print) | LCC PZ7.1.A4357 (eBook) | DDC [E]—dc23
LC record available at https://lccn.loc.gov/2018051370

Our Favorite Day of the Year

WRITTEN BY

A. E. Ali

ILLUSTRATED BY

Rahele Jomepour Bell

SALAAM
READS

NEW YORK LONDON TORONTO
SYDNEY NEW DELHI

On Musa's very first day of kindergarten, his teacher, Ms. Gupta, said, "Look around the room. You don't know them now, but these faces will become your closest friends this year."

Musa looked at the three boys at his table. They didn't look like his friends. They were total strangers.

"A great way to make new friends is by sharing things we like. For me, meeting new students is my favorite thing to do! That's why the first day of school is my favorite day of the year."

Musa couldn't believe that was true. And he could tell Moisés, Mo, and Kevin didn't believe it either.

"This year for show-and-tell, you will take turns telling us all about your favorite day of the year. That way throughout the year the class will celebrate it with you!"

Musa perked up at this. The best day of the year was definitely Eid! Surely Eid was *everyone's* favorite day.

Musa sat with Moisés, Mo, and Kevin at lunch.

"I don't get it," said Mo. "The first day of school?
How can it be anyone's favorite?"

"How can it be more fun than *Christmas*?"
said Moisés.

"My family doesn't celebrate Christmas," said Musa.

"Me neither," said Mo and Kevin.

"My favorite holiday is coming up," said Musa.
"Maybe we'll celebrate at school!"

A few weeks later, Musa and his mom brought in food and decorations for the class.

EID MUBARAK, said the sign.

Musa taught the kids how to say it.

"On Eid al-Fitr my family goes to the mosque to pray early in the morning, and afterward we have a HUGE breakfast. Family and friends come to the house all day, to eat food and bring presents.

"People eat all kinds of food, since Muslims come from around the world." Musa shared malawax, youxiang, and rose lassi.

Everyone could see why Eid was Musa's favorite.

Soon it was Mo's turn.

SHANAH TOVAH, said the sign.

Mo stood at the front of the classroom and said, "Happy New Year!
My family is preparing for the Jewish New Year of Rosh Hashanah!"

Mo taught the kids how to say it.

"On Rosh Hashanah we light candles at night, and go to the synagogue during the day with our family and friends. We also eat lots of yummy food for a sweet new year, and wish each other Shanah Tovah."

Mo brought apples dipped in honey and challah bread to share with the class.

Everyone could see why Rosh Hashanah was Mo's favorite.

During winter it was Moisés's turn.

"FELIZ NAVIDAD," said Moisés.
"I'm sure you guys have heard of Christmas,
but not the way my family celebrates!

"On Christmas we celebrate Las Posadas."

Moisés taught the kids how to say it.

"It lasts nine days, and we decorate the house with flowers, wreaths, and lanterns. We sing songs, drink ponche navideño, and hit a piñata! On the ninth day, Buena Noche, we go to church at midnight, and open presents when we get home."

Moisés brought ponche navideño and a piñata for the class.

Everyone could see why Christmas was Moisés's favorite.

That spring, it was Kevin's turn!

"HAPPY PI DAY," said the class.

"My family celebrates science," said Kevin. "Pi Day is on March fourteenth, because 3.14 is a very important number in math. On that day, my family makes different kinds of pies and we learn about scientists and their discoveries. This year, we learned about volcanoes."

Kevin shared what he had learned.

Kevin also shared about his favorite scientist, Isaac Newton,
who discovered gravity when an apple fell on his head.

Kevin brought freshly baked apple pie to share with the class.

Everyone could see why Pi Day was his favorite.

On the last day of school, their teacher sat the class down in a circle. "I'm going to miss you all very much," she said. "I want you to look around the classroom."

Musa looked and saw his best friends,
Moisés, Mo, and Kevin, and the other
kids he'd gotten to know this year.

But what if Musa, Moisés, Mo, and Kevin weren't in the same class next year?

Their teacher handed out a calendar with many holidays on it.

"This way you can always remember when we're not together to celebrate the days that brought us together!"

The whole year was full of days to
celebrate with friends, new and old.

LEARN MORE ABOUT THE HOLIDAYS
MUSA, MOISÉS, MO, AND KEVIN
SHARE TOGETHER!

EID AL-FITR is a Muslim holiday that marks the end of the Islamic month of Ramadan. During Ramadan, Muslims like Musa's family fast from sunrise to sundown. On Eid, families often go to the mosque to pray together and share meals with their community.

ROSH HASHANAH is the beginning of the Jewish New Year. It is a fall holiday, often taking place in September or October. Many Jewish families like Mo's celebrate by eating challah bread or apples dipped in honey to symbolize a sweet start to their year.

LAS POSADAS is a Christian holiday that honors the birth of Jesus by celebrating the nine days leading up to Christmas. Las Posadas is a tradition observed in many Latin American countries, including Mexico, which is where Moisés's grandparents are from.

PI DAY is a holiday that honors an important number: 3.14. This number is called "pi" and it is essential to measuring circles. Pi Day is not a widely celebrated holiday, but in recent years many people, including Kevin's parents, like to celebrate math and science on that day because the date March 14 corresponds with the number 3.14.

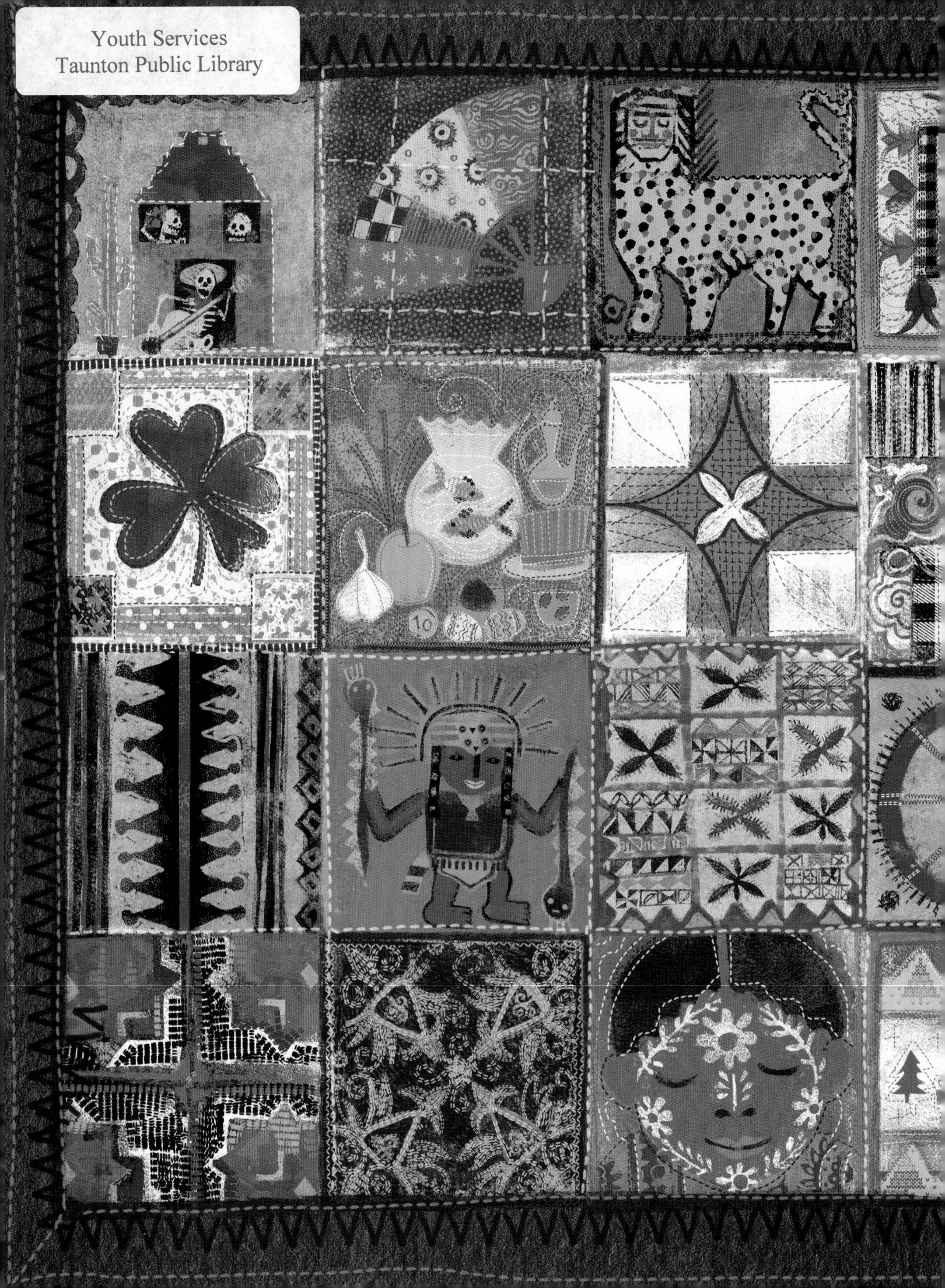
10